POLLINATOR PALS
BENITO THE BAT POLLINATES

by Rebecca Donnelly
illustrated by Dean Gray

GRASSHOPPER

Tools for Parents & Teachers

Grasshopper Books enhance imagination and introduce the earliest readers to fiction with fun storylines and illustrations. The easy-to-read text supports early reading experiences with repetitive sentence patterns and sight words.

Before Reading

- Discuss the cover illustration. What do they see?
- Look at the glossary together. Discuss the words.

Read the Book

- Read the book to the child, or have him or her read independently.
- "Walk" through the book and look at the illustrations. Who is the main character? What is happening in the story?

After Reading

- Prompt the child to think more. Ask: Benito the bat needs agave nectar for food. Agave plants need lesser long-nosed bats like Benito to help them reproduce. Can you think of other plants and animals that rely on one another?

Grasshopper Books are published by Jump!
5357 Penn Avenue South
Minneapolis, MN 55419
www.jumplibrary.com

Copyright © 2022 Jump! International copyright reserved in all countries. No part of this book may be reproduced in any form without written permission from the publisher.

Library of Congress Cataloging-in-Publication Data

Names: Donnelly, Rebecca, author.
Gray, Dean, illustrator.
Title: Benito the bat pollinates / by Rebecca Donnelly; illustrated by Dean Gray.
Description: Minneapolis, MN: Jump!, Inc., [2022]
Series: Pollinator pals
Includes reading tips and supplementary back matter.
Audience: Ages 7-10.
Identifiers: LCCN 2021000227 (print)
LCCN 2021000228 (ebook)
ISBN 9781636902227 (hardcover)
ISBN 9781636902234 (paperback)
ISBN 9781636902241 (ebook)
Subjects: LCSH: Readers (Primary)
Leptonycteris–Juvenile fiction.
Classification: LCC PE1119.2 .D6695 2022 (print)
LCC PE1119.2 (ebook)
DDC 428.6/2–dc23
LC record available at https://lccn.loc.gov/2021000227
LC ebook record available at https://lccn.loc.gov/2021000228

Editor: Eliza Leahy
Direction and Layout: Anna Peterson
Illustrator: Dean Gray

Printed in the United States of America at Corporate Graphics in North Mankato, Minnesota.

Table of Contents

A Midnight Snack	4
Let's Review!	22
Where Lesser Long-Nosed Bats Live	23
To Learn More	23
Glossary	24
Index	24

A Midnight Snack

Good evening! My name is Benito. I'm a lesser long-nosed bat. I am nocturnal. That means I am active at night.

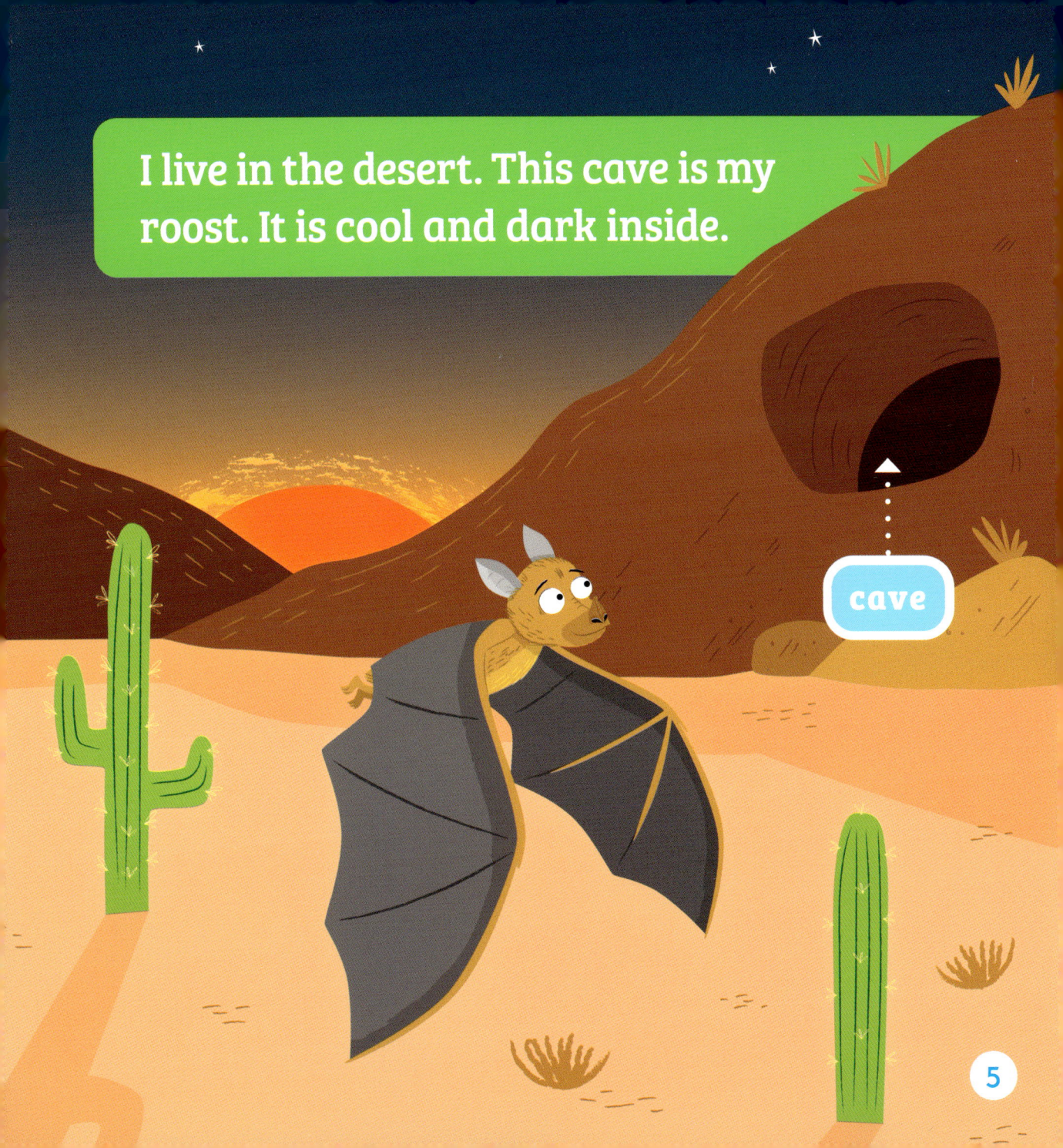

I live in the desert. This cave is my roost. It is cool and dark inside.

cave

I sleep here all day with thousands of other male bats. The female bats and babies in our colony roost in a cave nearby.

We hang upside down while we sleep. We grip the rocky ceiling with our toes. We wrap our wings around our bodies.

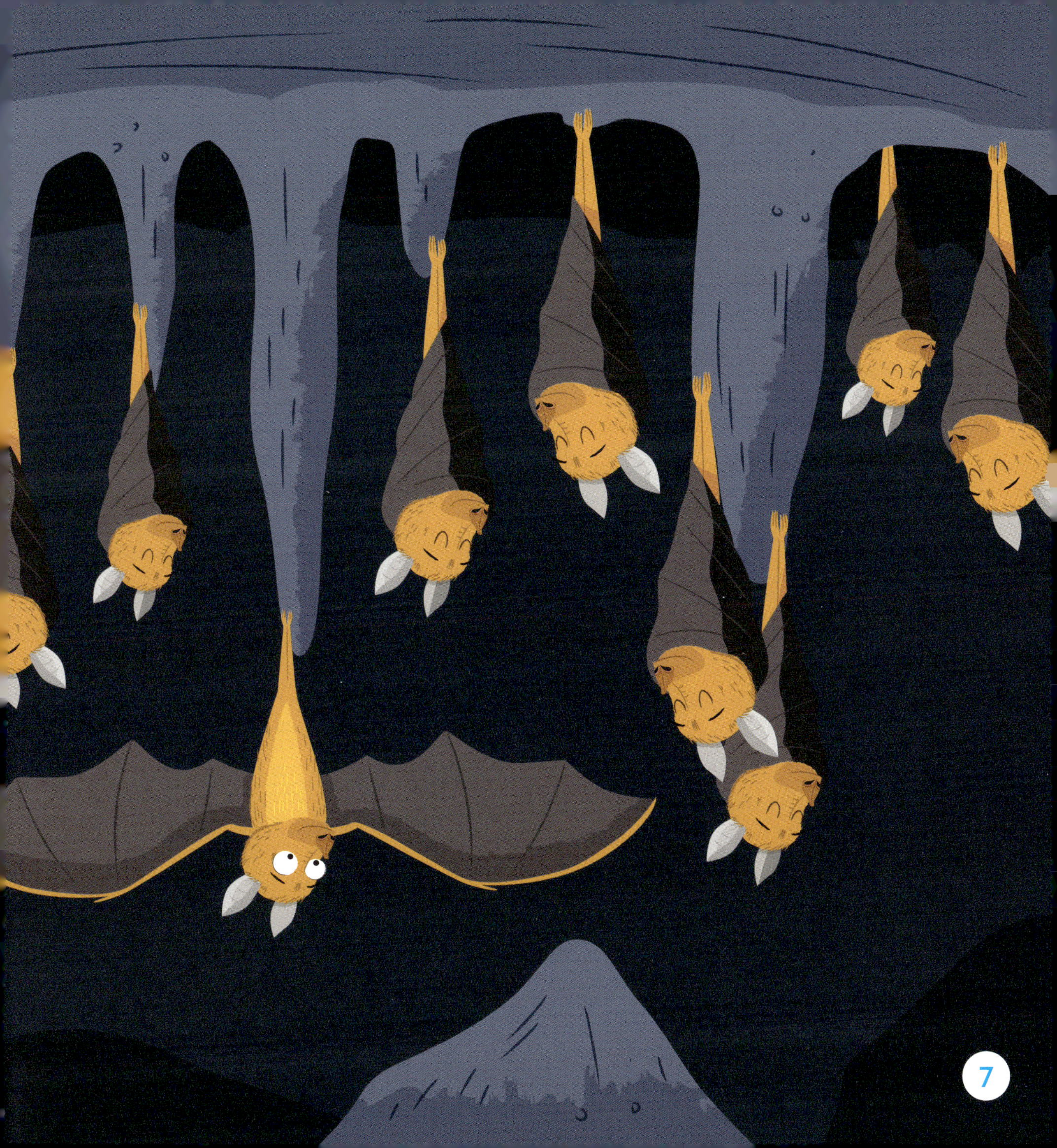

Bats are the only mammals that can fly! When the sun goes down, we fly across the desert to look for food.

Other kinds of bats eat insects. But we fly in search of nectar. It is getting dark. Let's go!

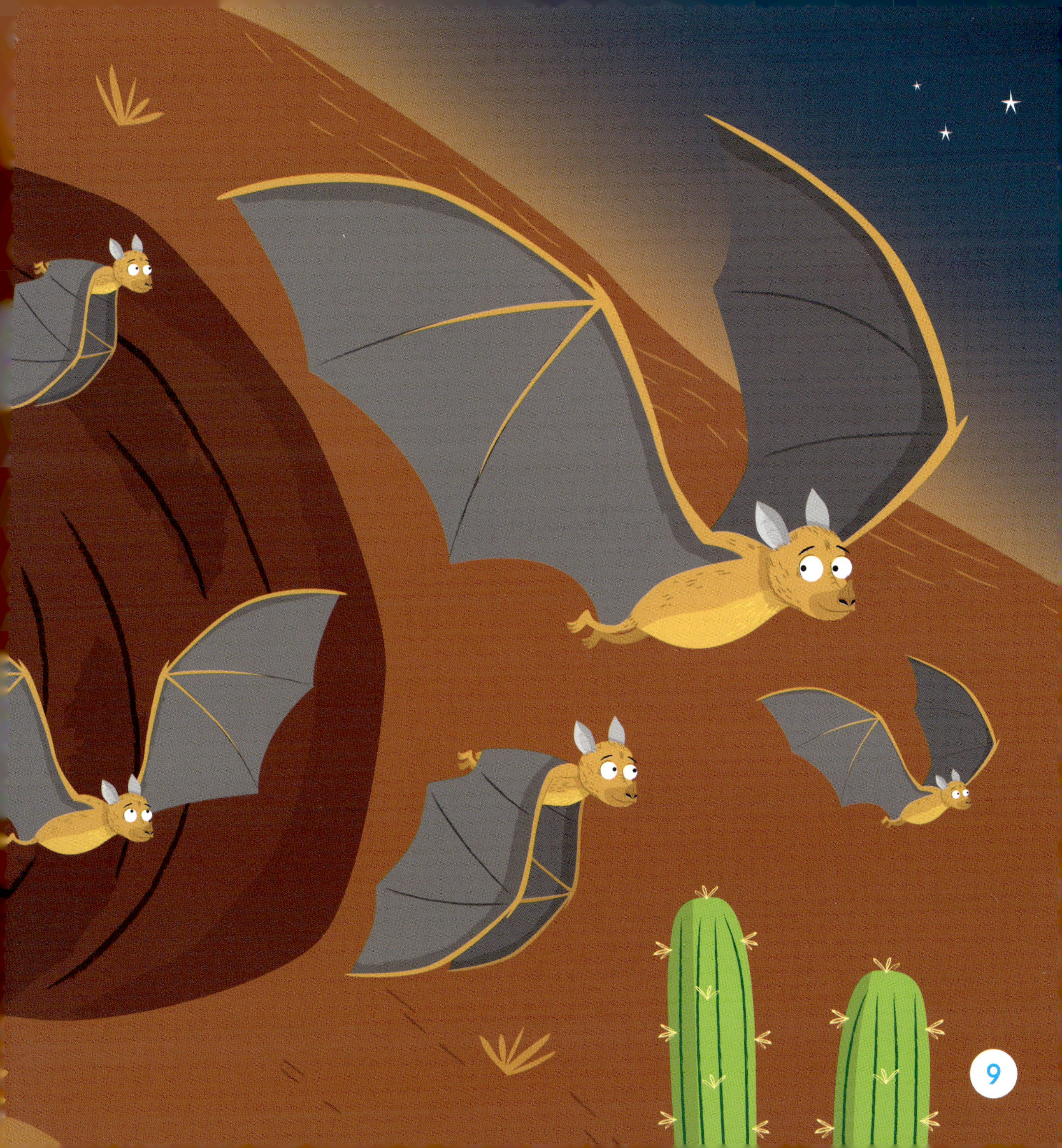

We love nectar from agave and cactus flowers. They bloom at night, so it's easy for us to drink their nectar.

cactus flower

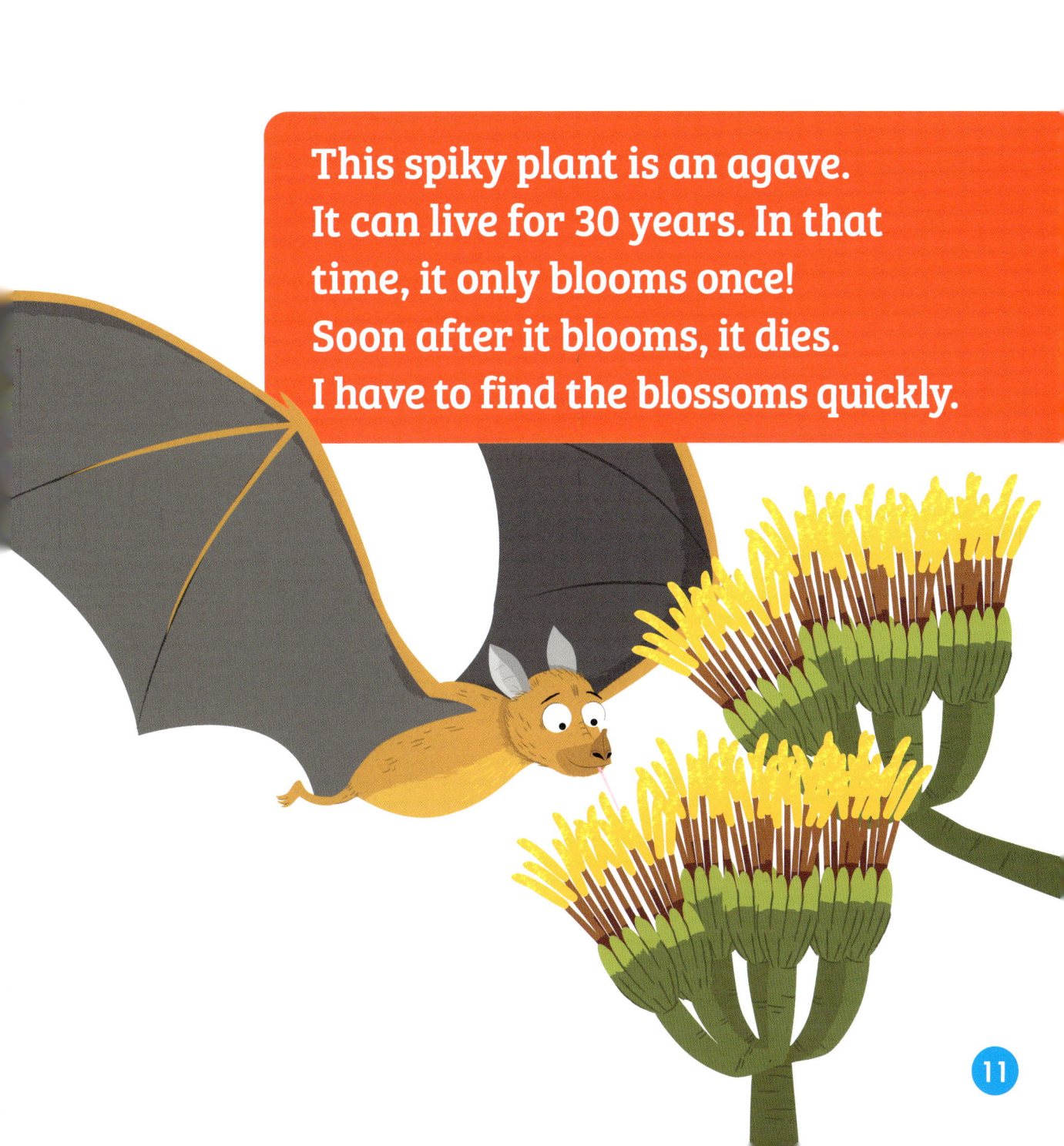

This spiky plant is an agave. It can live for 30 years. In that time, it only blooms once! Soon after it blooms, it dies. I have to find the blossoms quickly.

My nose helps me find food. I have a very good sense of smell. I also make clicking sounds with my nose. My nose leaf helps send out sound waves. The waves bounce off flowers. This is called echolocation. It helps me find flowers in the dark!

nose leaf

13

My tongue is as long as my body. It reaches into flowers. I can visit 100 flowers in one night! Pollen sticks to my fur.

pollen

I fly to another agave. The pollen on my fur sticks to the blossoms. That is how I pollinate! When a plant is pollinated, it makes seeds. Seeds grow into new plants.

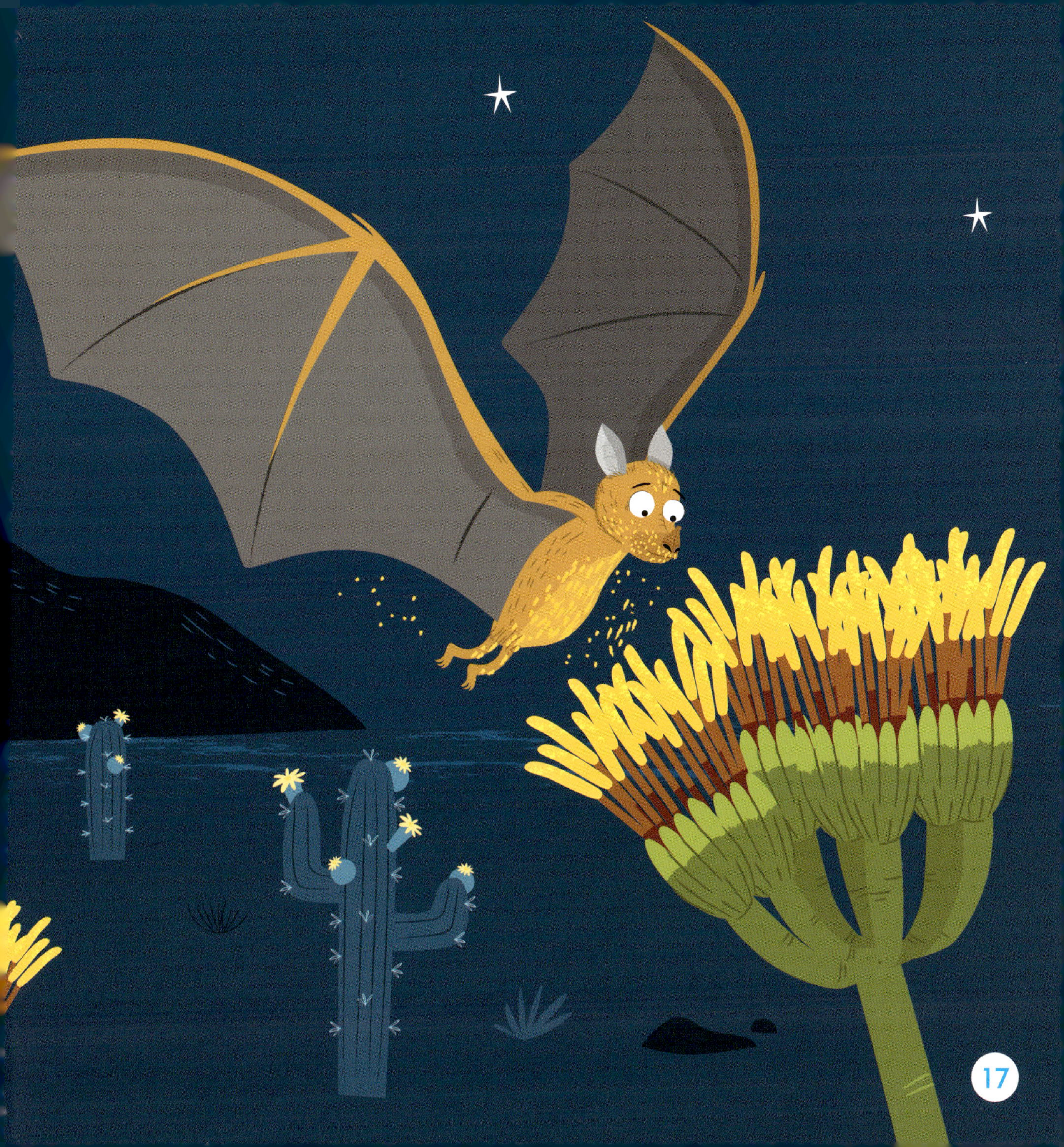

I pollinate saguaros and organ pipe cacti, too.

saguaro ┄┄▶ organ pipe cactus ┄┄▶

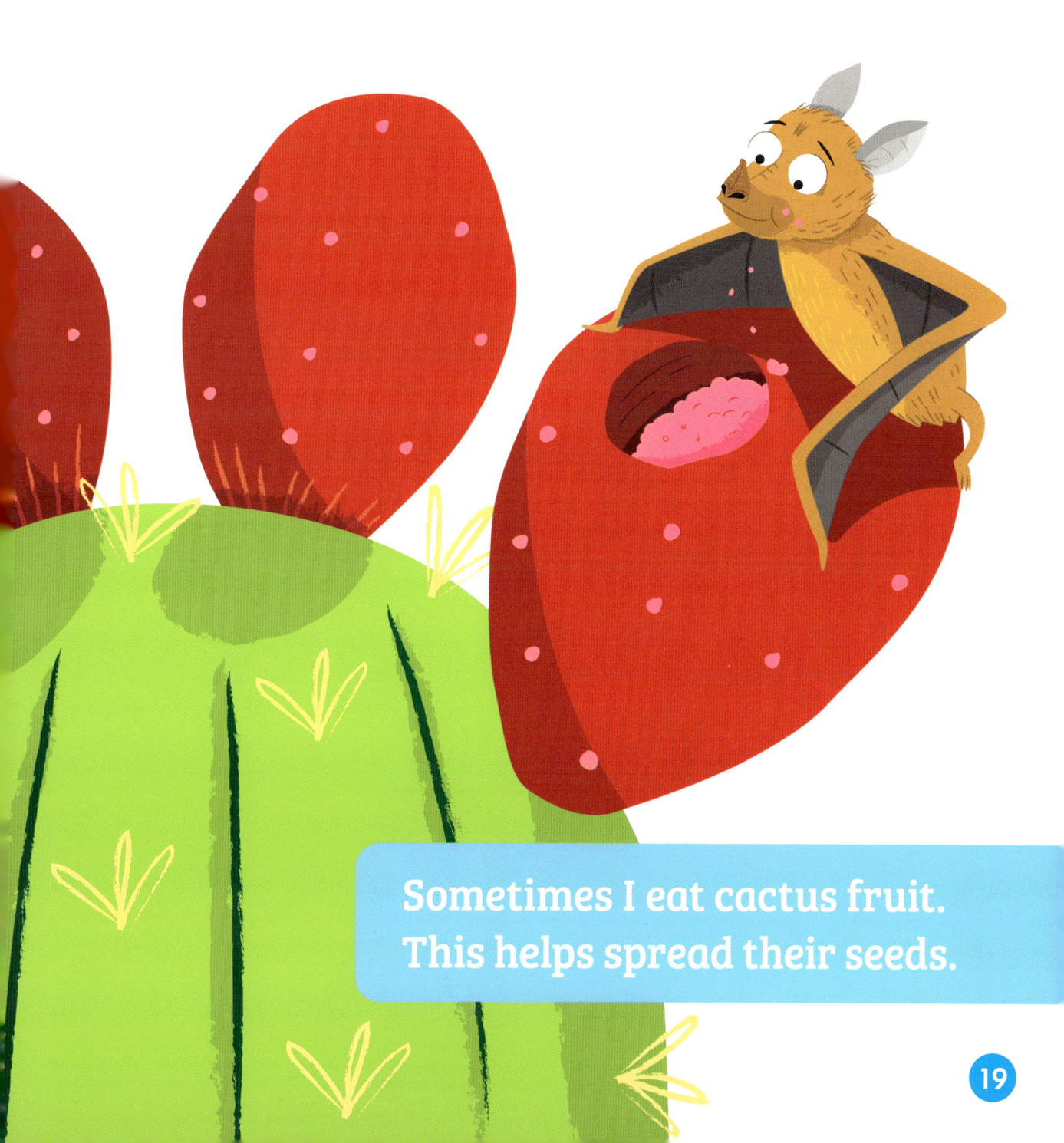

Sometimes I eat cactus fruit.
This helps spread their seeds.

Soon my colony will need to find more food. We will migrate south and look for a new roost.

But for now, the sun is rising. Time to get some sleep!

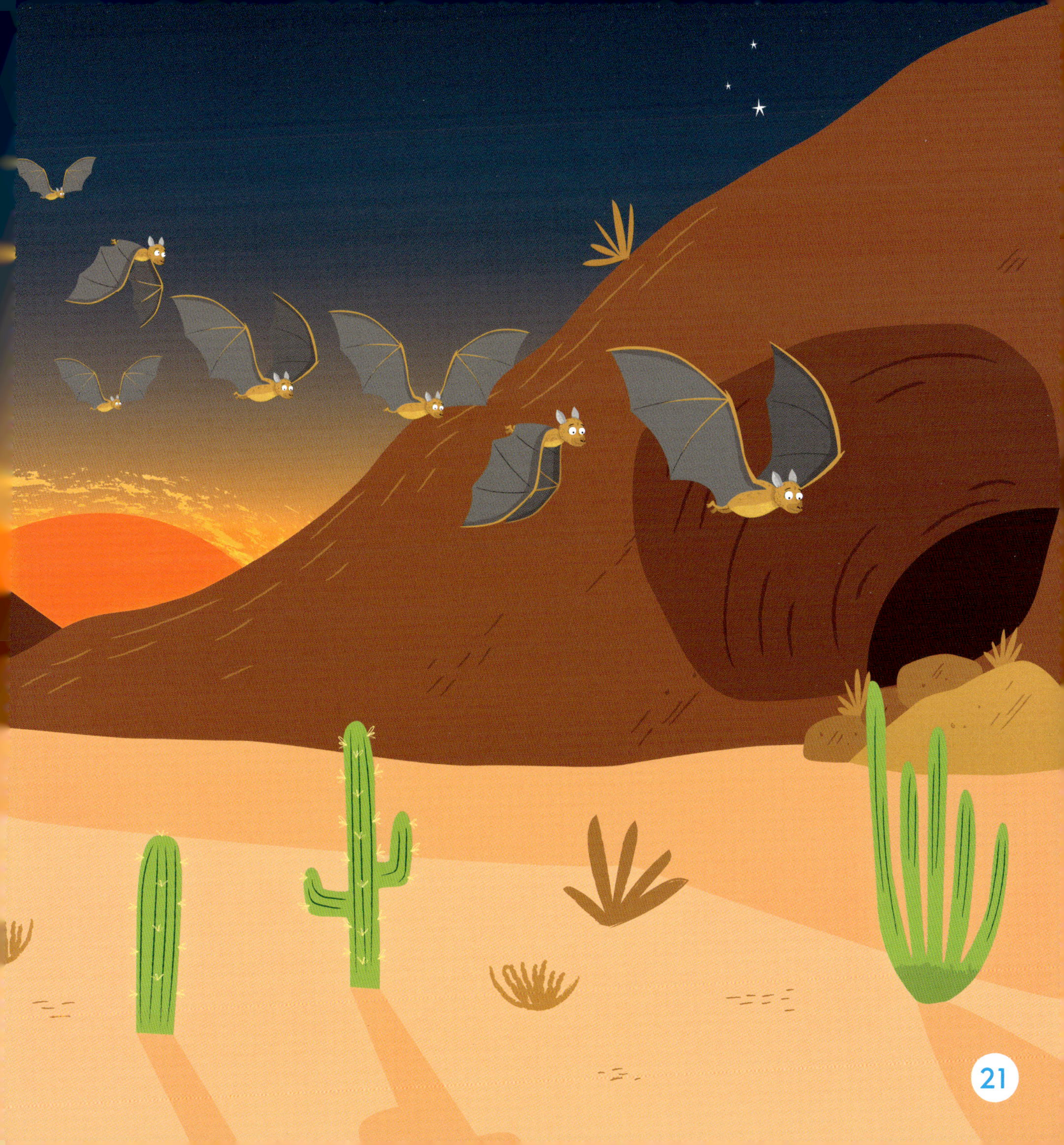

Let's Review!

Agave and cactus plants need help from lesser long-nosed bats to reproduce. Let's take a look at how Benito pollinates these plants.

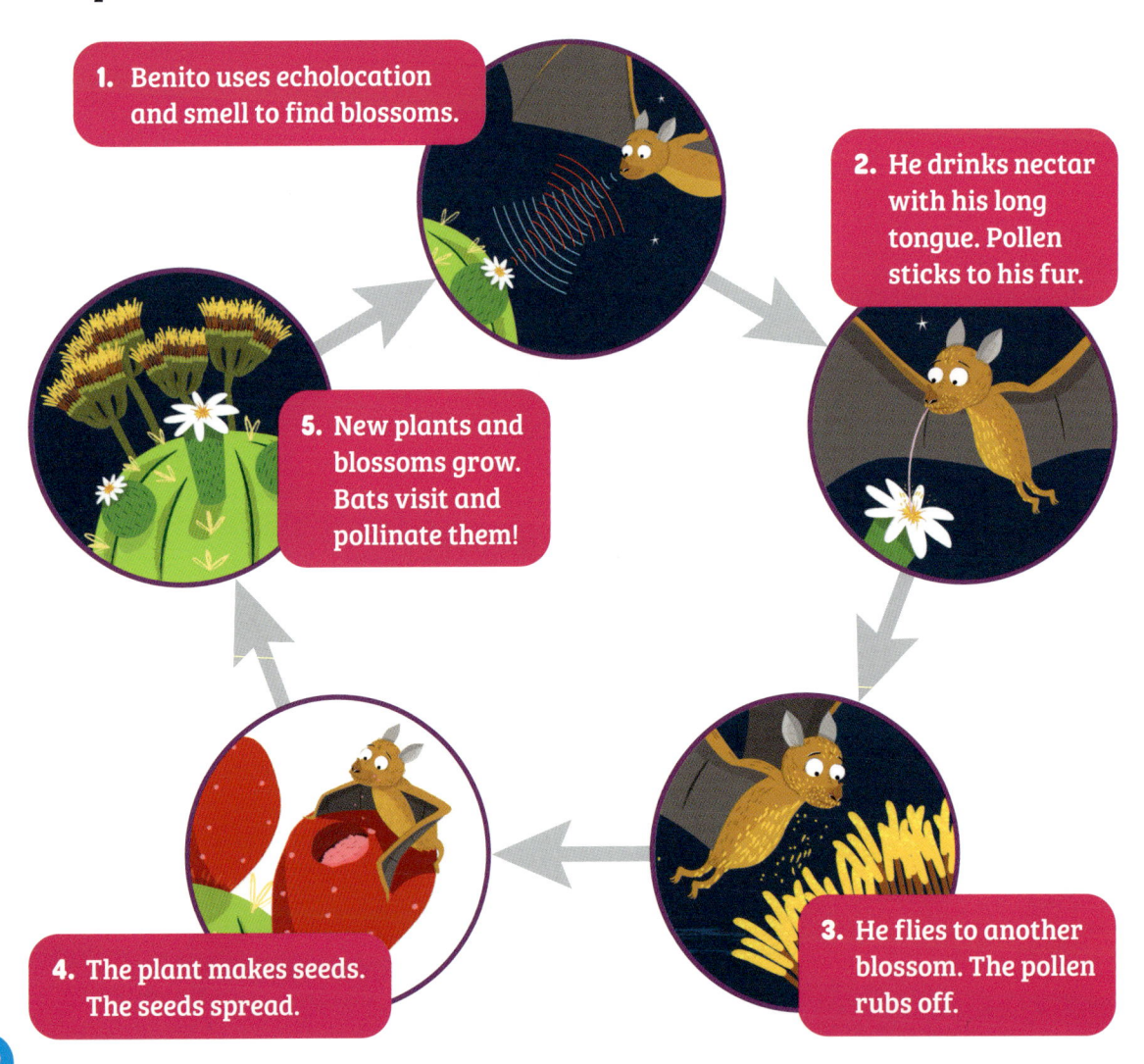

1. Benito uses echolocation and smell to find blossoms.

2. He drinks nectar with his long tongue. Pollen sticks to his fur.

3. He flies to another blossom. The pollen rubs off.

4. The plant makes seeds. The seeds spread.

5. New plants and blossoms grow. Bats visit and pollinate them!

Where Lesser Long-Nosed Bats Live

Benito is a lesser long-nosed bat. These bats are found in Mexico and the southwestern United States. Take a look!

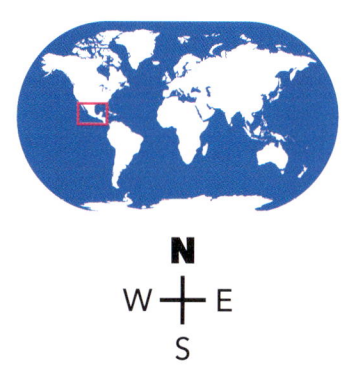

To Learn More

Finding more information is as easy as 1, 2, 3.

1. Go to www.factsurfer.com
2. Enter "**Benitothebatpollinates**" into the search box.
3. Choose your book to see a list of websites.

Glossary

blossoms: Flowers on trees and bushes.

colony: A group of bats that lives together.

echolocation: Using sound to find objects. When a bat makes a click with its mouth or nose, the sound waves bounce off objects and back to the bat's ears.

mammals: Warm-blooded animals that have fur and give birth to live babies.

migrate: To move to another area or climate at a particular time of year.

nectar: A sweet liquid made by flowers to attract pollinators.

nose leaf: A flap of skin on a bat's snout that helps to direct sound waves in echolocation.

pollen: A powder made by the male parts of plants.

pollinate: To take pollen from the male part of a flower and put it on the female part of a flower so the plant can reproduce.

roost: A place where bats sleep together at night; to sleep in a group with other bats.

sound waves: Series of vibrations in the air, in a solid, or in a liquid that can be heard.

Index

agave 10, 11, 16

cactus 10, 18, 19

cave 5, 6

colony 6, 20

desert 5, 8

echolocation 12

flowers 10, 12, 14

fly 8, 16

nectar 8, 10

nose 12

pollen 14, 16

pollinate 16, 18

roost 5, 6, 20

sleep 6, 20

tongue 14

wings 6